AROUND THE WORLD with Matt & Lizzy

NIGERIA

YOU ARE WELCOME

CLUB1040.com Kids Mission series

Written by Julie Beemer   Illustrated by Guy Wolek

 **his Book Belongs To World Traveler,**

Psalm 112:2 (NIV)

Their children will be mighty in the land; The generation of the upright will be blessed.

CLUB1040 Kids Mission Series
Around The World with Matt and Lizzy

By Julie Beemer

Edited by Dagny Griffin

In addition to buying office supplies and eating avocados, Ms. Dagny loves making stories sparkle. That's why she's an editor. There is also something else she loves; an amazing kind of people called Christian writers, and one day she hopes to be one of them as well. Ms. Dagny has two children, two grandchildren, no cats and entirely too many books.

Illustrated by Guy Wolek

Guy has been drawing since he was a child and has never stopped. He has always had a love for developing characters and people's faces which brought him to illustrating children's books. He still loves creating characters and also enjoys teaching others how to find a face in a cloud.

Pictures & words put in place by Paul Thompson

From his early scribbles on the wallpaper of his parents' house, to his slightly more grown-up colouring-in as a graphic designer, he has always liked to create interesting visual things. He's also created one wonderful daughter, who has now made him a Gramps, too. And he still likes to play with pictures...

Dedicated to all our faithful staff, students, alumni and friends at Rhema Nigeria.

Acknowledgment

Thank you to all the wonderful parents, grandparents, aunts and uncles, pastors, and educators who purchase and promote our Around the World with Matt and Lizzy books. Because of you, children will be inspired to become global leaders, taking the gospel around the world and accomplishing God's plan for their lives. It thrills my heart when I see the photos of your children enjoying this book series. You can post their photos on

Facebook: Around The World with Matt and Lizzy
Instagram: @mattandlizzy

Special thanks to Matt and Julie Hattabaugh and Jasmyne Wisniewski for making this project a success.

A very special thanks to my daughter Elisabeth for making this book come alive. You can view a video of her in the actual Nigerian village at www.MattandLizzy.com.

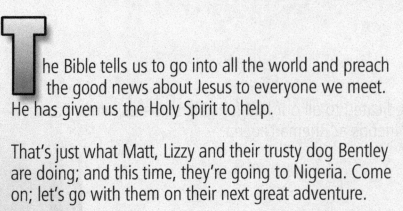

The Bible tells us to go into all the world and preach the good news about Jesus to everyone we meet. He has given us the Holy Spirit to help.

That's just what Matt, Lizzy and their trusty dog Bentley are doing; and this time, they're going to Nigeria. Come on; let's go with them on their next great adventure.

Destination: **ABUJA, NIGERIA - AFRICA**

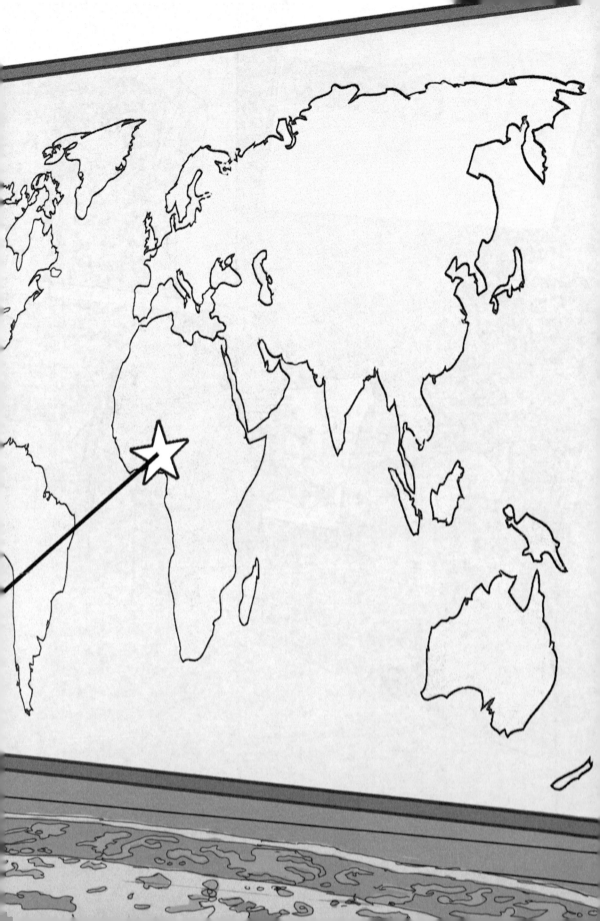

"**W**hen our Nigerian friends, Toks and Akunna, told us about an African village without clean drinking water, we wanted to help," explained Matt.

"We asked God how to raise enough money to dig a well. Pastor, the money your church has given for the well means we can all show the people in that village how much God really cares about them. Thank you so much! It is perfect timing, too, because Lizzy and I leave for Nigeria early tomorrow morning."

"Lizzy, stop fooling around! You're supposed to be packing," Matt scolded.

"I was until I got tangled up in this silly mosquito net," cried Lizzy. "Do I really have to bring it?"

"Yes," Matt said, trying to help Lizzy get free. "In Nigeria, there are mosquitos that carry malaria. If they bite you, it can make you very sick."

"Are you serious?" Lizzy said, with a squeamish look. "Maybe we shouldn't go!"

"Lizzy, the village needs their clean drinking water. Plus, you have no reason to be afraid. Remember what God's Word says about His protection and don't forget about the shots we got from the doctor?" Matt reminded.

"How could I forget?" Lizzy groaned, as she unwrapped her left foot from the net.

"God's Word, the shots and this mosquito net will keep us safe, right?" Lizzy questioned, finally free as she lifted the last of the net over her head.

"Of course," Matt smiled. "Now you and Bentley finish packing and get some sleep. And don't forget your passport!"

"Okie Dokie," Lizzy said, interrupted with a huge yawn.

Early the next day, Matt, Lizzy and their dog Bentley boarded the airplane headed for Nigeria. Matt and Bentley settled in quickly; Lizzy didn't.

"Ugh! This seat is so uncomfortable. How long is it going take to get there?" Lizzy complained.

"About twenty hours," Matt stated.

"Twenty hours! That's like forever!" Lizzy said, squirming in her seat and trying desperately to get comfortable.

"Not quite forever. And we are changing planes in London," Matt added.

Lizzy sat up straight. "London? Maybe we can see our friends, Ali and Rosie?"

"There won't be enough time," Matt said. Then he looked at his watch. "Speaking of time, make sure to change your watch. Let's see, it's 6:00 am here? That makes it lunchtime in Nigeria. It makes me hungry just thinking about it!"

"How can you think of food, Matt?" said Lizzy, as she pulled the blindfold over her eyes, "All that matters is my beauty sleep."

"**T**oks! Akunna!" Matt called, as he stepped out of the airport into the hot African air.

"Welcome, welcome!" said Toks, giving Matt a hearty hug. "Wait. You're alone? Where are Lizzy and Bentley?"

"Bentley was having some problems getting through customs," said Matt.

"Yes, even dogs must have their visas in order to come to Nigeria!" Toks said jokingly.

"Hopefully it won't take — ah, here they come!"

Lizzy and Bentley came out of the airport, but stopped short when they saw all the people waiting. Lizzy's heart started pounding, as all the new sights and sounds overwhelmed her.

"Over here!" Matt said, waving his hands in the air. Bentley saw Matt first and ran to meet him, while Lizzy tried to keep up.

"Welcome to Nigeria," said Akunna, as she embraced Lizzy with a big hug.

"Whew! I thought I was lost there for a minute!" said Lizzy, looking around. "There's so many people here."

"Nigeria has more people than any other country in Africa," said Akunna.

"And now it has two more," Matt said, laughing at how happy Bentley was to see him.

"And one more dog," Lizzy reminded them. "Right, Bentley?" Bentley agreed, wagging his tail at full speed!

"These city gates are the official entry to Abuja, our capital city," explained Akunna.

"Why are there so many kids running around in the middle of the road?" gasped Lizzy. "Don't they know they could get hit by a car?"

"This is how they make money," Akunna explained. "They sell food and drinks and other things to people waiting in traffic."

"Look at that, Matt," Lizzy said excitedly. "Instead of going through a drive-thru, the food comes to us!"

"What else is there to know about Nigeria, Toks?" Matt said.

Toks thought for a minute. "Even though we have big cities, there are still tribes here. I am from the Yoruba tribe."

"But I thought tribes people wore a lot of facepaint and crazy kinds of clothes?" Lizzy said.

Akunna laughed. "I hope not; I am from the Igbo tribe. Do I have crazy facepaint on?"

"No," Lizzy said, "but that's what I saw on TV."

"There may be a few small tribes like that still, but Nigeria is a very modern country with modern cities," Toks explained.

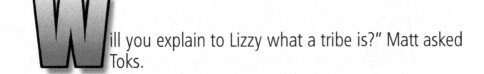

"**W**ill you explain to Lizzy what a tribe is?" Matt asked Toks.

"A tribe is just a big family with the same language, customs, and beliefs. There are hundreds of tribes in Nigeria and in the cities, you meet people from different tribes every day."

Lizzy blushed with embarrassment. "I guess sometimes you don't really know about people until you meet them."

YOU ARE WELCOME

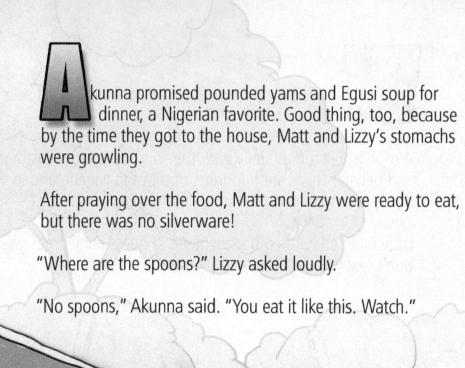

kunna promised pounded yams and Egusi soup for dinner, a Nigerian favorite. Good thing, too, because by the time they got to the house, Matt and Lizzy's stomachs were growling.

After praying over the food, Matt and Lizzy were ready to eat, but there was no silverware!

"Where are the spoons?" Lizzy asked loudly.

"No spoons," Akunna said. "You eat it like this. Watch."

Akunna picked up a piece of white doughy food from a nearby plate. "First you take some pounded yam and roll it into a ball."

"That is pounded yam?" Lizzy said. "It feels like sticky mashed potatoes."

"Except not so squishy," Matt said, also grabbing a small piece and rolling it into a ball.

"Now, dip the ball into your soup like this, and scoop," Akunna said. "Then you eat."

"Mmm, delicious!" said Matt, licking his fingers with delight.

"Plus, we can eat with our fingers without getting into trouble," Lizzy said, letting Bentley lick some of the sticky yam off of her fingers. "I love this country!"

"Just wait until you see the market," Toks said.

Arriving at the local market the next morning, Akunna told Matt and Lizzy, "This is where we buy our food and other things we need."

"How does she do that?" queried Lizzy, pointing to a woman balancing a plateful of oranges on her head.

"We learn that as part of our games when we are very little," said Akunna. "I can teach you how, if you want."

"I'm kind of a klutz," said Lizzy. "Oranges would be rolling all over the floor!"

"No," Akunna said. "You can do it; it just takes practice. Anyone can learn."

"But not right now. Are you ready to get a new dress, Lizzy?" Toks asked.

"A new dress?" she asked. "Of course!"

"We love to give our guests the gift of traditional clothing. Akunna and I want to give you a Nigerian dress for church this Sunday," Toks said.

"Really? Yay!" Lizzy squealed, bouncing up and down and rocking the keke.

"Zibah's Tailor Shop, please," Toks said to the keke's driver.

Zigzags, swirls and eye-popping colors covered every inch of Zibah's Tailor Shop: yellows and golds, greens and blues and more patterns and designs than Lizzy had ever seen.

"Choose your favorite Lizzy and Zibah will have a beautiful dress ready for you by tomorrow," Akunna stated.

Lizzy hemmed and hawed. "Hmm, I like this one the best! No, this one… wait — maybe… Matt, what do you think?"

Matt shrugged. "I think you should get whichever one you like."

"But that's the problem," Lizzy said. "I like them all!"

"It sounds like this may take a while," Toks said to Matt. "What do you say we go get some puff-puffs?"

"Great idea!" Matt said. "We'll meet you girls out in front of this store in half an hour."

"**M**att, Matt!" cried Lizzy.

"Hmm?" Matt groaned. He was half-asleep.

"There's a mosquito buzzing around my net and I don't want to get bit!"

Matt propped himself up on one elbow. "Lizzy, remember what the Bible says in Philippians 4:6: 'Don't worry about anything —' "

"Instead, pray about everything," Lizzy said. "Tell God what you need and thank Him for all He has done!"

"That's right," affirmed Matt. "We've done our part to be safe, and we've prayed. Now we trust God to take care of us."

It was quiet for a minute until Lizzy started singing a song from her heart:

"I won't worry, I won't fear.
My Bible tells me you are near.
Thank you God, you heard me pray,
So keep mosquitos far away!"

"That's the way!" Matt said, rolling over with a smile. "Now go to sleep, and just think of all the kids we get to help in the village tomorrow!"

Lizzy kissed Bentley goodnight and hummed her song until she fell into a deep, peaceful sleep.

They arrived in the village very early in the morning. Matt and Toks grabbed some tools while Lizzy and Akunna unloaded gifts for the villagers.

Suddenly, all the children crowded around them. Lizzy didn't know what to do; but then God's wisdom came into her heart.

"Akunna, let's sing that song you were teaching me!" Akunna and Lizzy started clapping and singing:
"Imela, Imela" (Thank you, Thank you)
"Okaka, Onyekeruwa" (Great and Mighty creator of the world)
"Imela, Imela" (Thank you, Thank you)
"Ezem oh" (My King)

Soon the children were singing and clapping, too and as they sang, Lizzy and Akunna handed out the gift bags.

Each bag contained fruit, pencils, candy, little toys and Christian comics in the Hausa language.

"Imela! Imela!" The children yelled and then sang even louder!

"Akunna, this is the best day ever!" announced Lizzy.

Meanwhile, Matt, Toks and Bentley went to see the workers that were helping to dig the borehole, which is what Nigerians call a well.

On their way toward the new borehole, Lizzy saw a little girl with a head covering. Lizzy wondered if the girl knew about Jesus.

"What is in her container?" Lizzy asked Akunna.

"Those are puff-puffs; it's like an African donut. She sells them to make money for her family. Would you like me to buy you one?"

"Yes," Lizzy said and Akunna gave the girl some money. The puff-puff tasted just like a really big donut-hole!

"Akunna, will you ask her if she knows about Jesus?" She said this because the girl didn't understand English. Most Nigerians in the big cities know English, but not always in the smaller villages.

Akunna asked the girl in her native Hausa language and the girl shook her head no. She had never even heard of Jesus.

"Will you tell her I will buy all of her puff-puffs if I can tell her about someone who loves her very much?"

Akunna told the girl and she was very excited. Not only did the little girl sell all of her puff-puffs, but she also learned about someone who loved her; someone called Jesus.

While Lizzy and Akunna talked to the puff-puff girl, Matt, Bentley and Toks helped with the new well for the village.

A drilling machine pounded loudly and dug a hole deep into the ground. Once the drilling was done, they put in a pump and suddenly, crystal clear drinking water poured out, like a fountain, from the top of the pipe. Everyone cheered!

"Let's thank the Lord for fresh water!" Toks said to all the people of the village. Matt and Toks prayed and afterward, everyone celebrated with singing and dancing!

O nce the water pump was finished, they went back to the marketplace to get Lizzy's dress.

"What an amazing day," Matt said, even though he was tired and sore from the work.

"Wasn't it?" Lizzy answered. All she could think about were the children's happy smiles and the puff-puff girl. Akunna and Lizzy had told her about Jesus and she asked Him into her heart; that made Lizzy very happy.

When they got to the tailor's shop, Zibah had the most beautiful dress waiting. Lizzy saw the price tag; it cost eight thousand naira, naira is the currency of Nigeria.

"It's so beautiful, Zibah. Thank you!" Lizzy reached into her purse to get some naira, but all she could find were puff-puffs. Her face turned red.

"Matt, can I borrow some of your naira? I spent all of my money on puff-puffs!"

"No need for that," Zibah said. "The dress is already paid for."

"But who paid for it?" Lizzy asked.

"Toks, of course," Akunna said. "It is his 'thank you' for coming all this way to help!"

"Thank you, Toks!" Lizzy said and gave him a big smile.

"Do you see that over there?" Toks said. He pointed through the window of the taxi.

"That huge mountain?" Matt asked.

"Oh that's not a mountain, that's Aso Rock," said Toks.

"When we see this rock, it means we are close to Abuja," added Akunna. "And the President of Nigeria lives close to that rock in the presidential palace."

"**W**ow, that's the biggest rock I've ever seen," stated Matt while also yawning.

"Does that mean we're almost back to your place?" Lizzy asked, trying hard to keep her eyes open.

"Almost," Akunna said.

By the time they reached Akunna's house, everyone was so tired they went straight to bed; but not before they took a few minutes to thank God for all He had done.

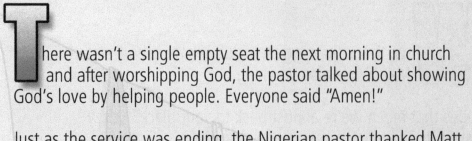

There wasn't a single empty seat the next morning in church and after worshipping God, the pastor talked about showing God's love by helping people. Everyone said "Amen!"

Just as the service was ending, the Nigerian pastor thanked Matt and Lizzy for coming and invited them to pray for those who had come to be born again. When they finished, the people who had been prayed for were so thankful and began to dance and sing like never before.

When it was time to go home. Toks and Akunna brought Matt, Lizzy and Bentley back to the airport.

"Thank you so much for everything," Matt said.

"No, no," Toks said. "Ese" (pronounced eshay).

"What does 'ese' mean?" Lizzy asked.

"That is how we say 'Thank you' in my Yoruba tribe," Toks said.

"In the Igbo tribe, we say 'Imela', like in the song you learned," Akunna said.

"Okay, ese and Imela," Matt said, "for taking care of us and helping us with the well. We couldn't have done all this without your help."

"We say the same to you! Thank you for showing God's love to that village."

Lizzy hugged Akunna. "Imela," she said.

"Thank you to you, too," Akunna said, "and please come back again."

Lizzy and Bentley were sad to leave Nigeria, but Matt cheered them up.

"Come on, you two," he said.

"Let's get home to find out what our next adventure is!"

COMING SOON

FROM CLUB1040 KIDS MISSION SERIES

Around the World with Matt and Lizzy – Egypt
Around the World with Matt and Lizzy – Mexico
Around the World with Matt and Lizzy – Wales
Around the World with Matt and Lizzy – Lebanon

You can order copies for our Around The World Mission Series by emailing mattandlizzy@club1040.com.

We would like to extend a special invitation to help write an adventure with Matt and Lizzy by emailing us at mattandlizzy@club1040.com.

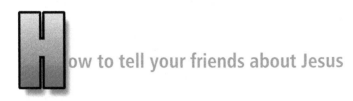

How to tell your friends about Jesus

If your friend wants to become a Christian, this is what you can say to him or her:

- Believe you have sinned against God (Romans 3:23).

- Say you are sorry for your sins and you want to stop doing wrong (Acts 3:19).

- Ask Jesus to forgive you and make your heart clean (Psalm 51:2,7).

- Trust Jesus to give you a new life that goes on forever (John 6:47).

- Tell Jesus you want to follow Him and let Him be Lord of your life and number one in your life (John 12:26).

A prayer your friend can pray:

"Dear God, I ask you to forgive me of my sin. I believe Jesus died on the cross and rose from the dead. I ask Jesus to live in my heart. Thank you. In Jesus' name, Amen."

If you or your friend have prayed this prayer, let Matt and Lizzy know and they will send you more information to help you grow in your new relationship with Jesus.

Email: mattandlizzy@club1040.com

Around The World with Matt and Lizzy Questions :

1   What has God told us to do around the world?

2   What did the church do to help send Matt and Lizzy to Nigeria?

3   What disease do some mosquitos carry in Nigeria?

4   What advice should you get from doctors before traveling to different countries?

5   How many hours ahead Is Nigeria from where you live?

6   What is the capital city of Nigeria?

7   What country has the most people in all of Africa?

8   What is a tribe?

9   What two tribes are Toks and Akunna from?

10 What were the children doing in the middle of the road?

11 What food did Lizzy eat with her hands?

12 What were the two forms of transportation that Matt and Lizzy used in Nigeria?

13 What do you call the person who made Lizzy a dress?

14 Are we supposed to worry about anything?

15 What does the Bible tell us to do when we are worried?

16 What did Lizzy do when she was scared of the mosquito?

17 Why did the village need a well?

18 What is the type of currency you use in Nigeria?

19 What is the name of the massive rock in Abuja?

20 What are the two different ways you can say 'Thank You' in Nigeria?

Lessons with Lizzy: What to do when you are worried

1. Don't speak words of worry; instead tell God exactly what you need.

2. Speak or sing out loud by thanking Him for everything He has done and will do, for you.

3. Remind yourself that God cares for you so much and wants your very best.

4. Trust that God's peace will steady the feelings in your heart and quiet all the thoughts in your head.

5. A helpful verse to memorize:

    Philippians 4:6-7 (NIV)

    Do not be anxious about anything, but in every situation, by prayer and petition, with thanksgiving, present your requests to God. And the peace of God, which transcends all understanding, will guard your hearts and your minds in Christ Jesus.

Bentley's Top Travel Tips

1   Drink lots of water while traveling, so bring an empty bottle from home to fill up past airport security. Drink only approved bottled water in the country you visit.

2   Bring electronic devices, chargers and entertainment, with proper adapters, for each country; check voltage on items and don't forget to color-code each person's charger cords.

3   Currency; take a minimum of $100 of the local currency.

4   Vaccinations and Medication; always check in advance with your family doctor about needed vaccinations and medicines required for each country.

5   Visa Information; always check if a visa is needed for each country.

6   Snacks; take lots of familiar snacks for long layovers and when food isn't to your liking.

7   Ziploc® Bags; use plastic baggies for packing all liquid items.

8   Zip Ties; pack lots of zip ties for bag security.

9   Make your bags easily distinguishable for overseas travel.

10   Do not pack any valuable items in checked in baggage.

igerian Puff Puff recipe

Ingredients

- 2 cups warm water
- 2¼ teaspoon active dry yeast (1 packet)
- 3½ cups flour
- 1/2- 3/4 cup sugar
- 1/2 tablespoon salt
- Oil for deep-frying

Instructions

Mix salt, sugar, water and yeast. Set aside for 5 minutes. Add flour and mix and let the mixture rise for approximately one to two hours.

In an electric skillet or deep-fat fryer, heat oil to 375°. Drop dough by heaping teaspoonfuls, five or six at a time, into oil.

Fry until browned, about one to two minutes, turning once. Drain on paper towels.

Roll warm puff-puffs in confectioners' sugar.

About CLUB1040.com

CLUB1040 is a relational missionary movement started by Matt and Julie Beemer in 1994. Their main purpose is to bring the Gospel to the least-reached areas of the 1040 window.

One of their passions is to inspire the church to fulfill the Great Commission in this generation. This book series is an outreach of CLUB1040 kids and is designed to inspire children to have God's heart for the world: while teaching practical travel tips, biblical truths and educational information about different countries.

CLUB1040.com is a non-profit organization. All proceeds of this mission book series go to inspiring and supporting families to reach their generation for Christ through CLUB1040.com.

CLUB1040 offers short-term mission adventures for teams and families. To be part of a CLUB1040 mission experience, or partner with CLUB1040.com, please go to www.club1040.com, or email us at admin@club1040.com.

You can also text CLUB1040 to 41444 to receive more information about CLUB1040.

CPSIA information can be obtained
at www.ICGtesting.com
Printed in the USA
LVOW06s0831300716

498359LV00002B/2/P